The Red Skull

Fiction novel

The Red Skull

Abdenal Carvalho

Summary

First Part

Survivors

During the winter a lot of garbage floated by the stream that passed under the stilts built by the riverside people inside the bags thrown by the residents of the upper parts of the city, it was such a huge amount that it caused astonishment for those who had the bad luck to live there.

At the end of the rains, when the thunderstorms finally ceased, it was hard work to remove all that dirt that was stuck in most of the pillars that supported the houses built in the water in the summer. The woman was not yet thirty years old, but she looked much older due to the exhausting life she was leading, she had almost no rest, she ate poorly and lost a lot of weight.

In one of those wooden huts rotted by the passage of time, there was a mother and son surviving as they could for several decades. Lucia and Pedro lived in a small hut, measuring about eight square meters.

Whose roof covered with old raw clay tiles dripped whenever winter came and the rains became more frequent. His daily routine was to leave his young son with his neighbor while doing various jobs in the homes of the rich in exchange for some changes that were barely enough to maintain his livelihood.

Things improved after the mayor had a small nursery built in the vicinity of the place that allowed mothers to leave their children there while they worked, so they studied and mothers still received a living allowance from the government to keep them in class. of class. She was encouraged by other mothers to enroll the boy.

— ... Yes, woman, put your son there who is already a great help! — Warned one of the residents

— For sure, I already enrolled my three boys! — added the other

— Okay, I will do as you are advising me, tomorrow I will ask the boss for leave and on Wednesday I miss the service to solve this

— Good idea, my neighbor, we don't give up these things!

The woman was not yet thirty years old, but she looked much older due to the exhausting life she was leading, she had almost no rest, she ate badly and lost a lot.He led an exhausting life, losing sleep when he had to work all day and when he returned in the evening still taking care of little Pedro and the organization of the old shack where they lived together.

She had become pregnant with the boy ten years before, during which time she was abandoned during the first months of pregnancy by her husband, who exchanged her for another. Since then, he had to assume a dual role in raising his son, acting as mother and father, thus duplicating his immense responsibility. The child's intelligence was notorious and he soon learned to read and write, was passionate about reading and was enchanted by the stories in his books.

Everything was going well, summer had come and the heavy rains were giving way to beautiful sunny mornings and, early in the morning, you could hear the birds singing on the tree branches, as they walked hand in hand with the mother towards the nursery. , where Aunt Lucia taught him to write new words and do math.

However, the unexpected happened that afternoon, when one of the drunken residents caused the fire in one of the shacks. The fire started under a strong blow of the winds that usually manifested itself there at that time and soon spread through all the other hovels at an incredible speed.

So fast was the action of the flames that barely enough time for some residents to manage to save their own life. All the stilts started to burn and the fire spread from one to the other in the blink of an eye. In a matter of minutes everything turned into a heap of ashes.

And when the fire brigade arrived with the intention of containing the fire it had already fulfilled its role to destroy everything he found ahead. At work Lucia received a call from a friend, warning her of the huge disaster that had occurred at her home. When he got there he only cared about hearing news from his son that nobody seemed to know the whereabouts, he only had peace when he heard from one of the residents that the child was safe.

— Calm down, neighbor, he's at home!

— Blessed be God, my neighbor, I almost died of fright!

— Don't worry, as soon as the panic started he had the idea of going to our house on the other side of the stream

— Yes, I always told him that if something bad happened to run to the residents' house on the other side of the small bridge

— Well, you did very well!

— And now, how will it be for us who lost everything?

— Bed, neighbor, everything will be fixed, you will see

— God hear you, because I have no idea how we're going to survive this

João was a widower, had lost his wife to cancer many years ago and always asked Lucia, who also lived alone in the struggle for survival. However, she never accepted her various proposals. However, on that desperate day, he had no choice but to agree to spend a season there.

Pedro loved the idea, because it was a large house, with several compartments and built in masonry, it seemed like a palace, since he grew up in that shabby rotten wood, climbed on four pillars and in the middle of the stinky stream where the excrement flowed. uptown staff, it was almost unbearable rot.

— Do not worry about the gossip, Lucia, we are free people and we have nothing to explain to these people. So, settle down with your child in one of the rooms and take charge of everything around here, pretend that the house is yours

— Thank you for your accommodation, João, I promise I will do my best not to take too much of your time, as soon as I find another place we vacate your house

— Stop it, woman, you know you don't need to be in such a hurry, if you want to accept my proposal or need to leave here.

Lucia responds to the elderly man's invitation with another yellow smile, showing little interest in accepting to be his companion.

At thirty-eight years old and completely disappointed in men, she no longer believed in love and completely lost a woman's desire. He knew that he would not be able to give her sexual pleasure and that it would become a major disappointment for a man who had several fantasies about her.

The very large place, with several rooms, delighted the boy who kept on praising his new home. The brand new fifty-four-inch LED television emblazoned on the wall, all wrinkled and painted in pearl yellow, the luxurious sofa set in the middle of the room, the two-door refrigerator, the stainless steel stove with six burners and so many other pieces of furniture. .Everything made the place the most beautiful place in the world in the eyes of little Pedro.

— Mom, everything here is very beautiful!

— Yes, my son, but remember that nothing here belongs to us

— Mom, why don't you marry Mr. João?

— What's this story, boy?

— There, mother, everyone here in the village knows that he likes you!

— Look how you say, little boy, have more respect!

— Fine...

The child was already able to understand the climate between the two adults and hoped that his mother would finally stop beating and accept the suitor's. Request, so that he could live better in such comfort, but his mother seemed to resist the obvious. After the fire in that part of the favela, the State Government and other non-governmental institutions decided to have new houses built for those people who had lost everything and a register was made to account for the damage and how many new houses had to be built to meet all families.

Lucia was one of the first to apply and started looking forward to the delivery of her new home. While he waited, he took care of his friend's residence and he worked at the free market in the neighborhood, where he owned several stalls selling fruit and vegetables. One day, tired of working only on domestic work and feeling the need to own her own money, she decided to propose something to the owner of the property.

— I want to ask you

— Yes, Lucia, talk

— I'm tired of being here washing, ironing, cooking ... I want to work on something where I can earn my own money

— But is something missing for you and your son, here?

— Of course not, you have met all our needs, even Pedro school supplies you give us, but I am used to earning my own living

— I understand, and what do you propose?

— You own several stalls at the fair, don't you?

— Certainly yes, why?

— What if you provided me with one of those vegetable stands so I could start working on it? So, at the end of the week or month, you would give me part of the profit and so I would have an activity that would earn me a salary instead of staying here as a domestic in this house

— Okay, if that's how you prefer ...

— Yes, I will feel more useful

— Okay, so tomorrow we start, you will take care of the stall where I have worked and I will just be managing the other fruit trees

— Okay, then

Lucia routine has changed since that new morning. Every day she woke up at dawn and went to the market to wait for João to arrive with his old car loaded with sacks of fruit and vegetables to be resold at his four stalls at the market.

After helping him distribute it among the other employees, she started to sell the products throughout the first hours of the day and at noon she went to the daycare in search of her son, who went with the mother to spend the rest of the afternoon at the sale.

On weekends João paid ten percent of everything he had earned with the new employee. And since she and little Pedro didn't have to spend what they received, he kept everything in a small box waiting to receive his new home and be able to buy some furniture there new.

It was many months since the fire set their homes on fire until finally the buildings were rebuilt and the residents, who were scattered throughout various places in the city, some in relatives' houses, others in schools and shelters, could return to tranquility from your own home.

During all this time John did everything to convince Lucia to at least sleep with him a few times, but the woman was resistant and her answer was always negative. Finally, after receiving the key to the new address, she thanked the elderly person for help and moved her son back to his space, where he could rest from the fatigue of living in others.

The new residence donated by the Government was not very large like João, but it was built in masonry and had a firm floor, all in concrete. The boy approved and jumped for joy. No one else lived on the edge of the stream nor on the high stilts built on tall, floating pillars on the slope of the manholes that flowed from the upper part of the city, where the rotten odors of the rich's excrement served as perfumes to the nostrils of the miserable poor.

They had been relocated to a drier area of the neighborhood and after the hovels were decimated to ash, the appearance of the place improved. There, a basic sanitation system was built to serve all families and no one else did their physiological needs in the open.

Air or play in the stream, everyone had a bathroom inside their homes and it was possible to maintain personal hygiene for the whole family. With the savings gained from her work at João fruit stand it was possible to survive even after moving, Lucia bought several new furniture, in addition to receiving donations from charitable people of various other household items.

Such as: Pans, dishes and all badly needed accessories in the kitchen. The financial situation of that woman improved after the immense disgrace that befell her life months ago, when she could not for the moment imagine herself as the owner of a property built entirely of bricks and covered with expensive ceramic tiles. Sometimes it takes a great deal of harm to befall someone's existence for things to change.

However, a time of good rain does not always correspond to a period of great harvests and she continued to work with João at the market stall while little Pedro studied at the new school built in the neighborhood and everything was going well.

However, that weekend something abnormal would happen again in the life of that family who seemed to be pursued by their own destiny. Mother and son went as usual very early to start their sales job at the fair and the boy.

Now eleven years old, had already adapted to that routine to the point of being quite useful in his chores.

Often he even took over for sale while his mother went to solve some external situation or take a look at the house that was locked up all day. But that morning, something had been planned for both of them and the time had come when mother and son should let go of their hands and he would learn to walk alone through the labyrinths of his existence.

Because a greater power decided to separate them much sooner than were expected. The narrow street that cut the fair almost forced the cars to bump into the stalls and run over those who traveled there, many trucks also circulated through the tight spot. They transported everything from fruits and vegetables to flammable products like butane gas, it was a real hell the movement there all day and the unexpected would happen.

Lucia ordered her son to go to the fruit stand across the narrow street to ask John for change for a high note because he was missing from the register. The boy was careless and paid little attention to the intense movement, crossing without looking closely both ways as his mother had warned him to do.

After only a few seconds when Pedro stepped away from his mother, the terrifying cry of one of the stallholders is heard for the boy to retreat in the face of the imminent danger that was approaching.

The woman, in a jump, got up from the small wooden bench where she sat and in a matter of seconds she was already in the middle of the narrow road with her son in her arms.

Her protective mother reflex prevented the high-speed garbage truck from hitting the child, but the impact of the crash was directly on her fragile body, hurling them both towards the sidewalk. The boy suffered some abrasions on his arms and legs, Lucia was already passed out and bleeding a lot.

After being properly rescued and taken to the emergency room, they were all assistants and by the friend the diagnosis was made by the doctors about his state of health, which was very serious, as he had broken both legs and one of his arms, lost blood in extreme and his condition was critical.

After the terrible accident, Lucia remained in the intensive care unit in critical condition for at least a month, during which time her son was taken care of by the neighbors, mainly João, who did not spare any effort for the brief recovery of his beloved. But, unfortunately, the boy's mother ended up not resisting his injuries and died.

That spring morning, when the scent of flowers on the trees was confused by that of the many roses and jasmines placed on the coffin where the inert body of that battling woman who gave her all to raise her only child alone and without the help of more, was found. no one, a boy of just eleven years of age.

Was preparing to continue his new journey without having his protector nearby. Pedro would have to be strong, follow his mother's example and not bow his head in the face of life's obstacles.

Never back down when confronted with what would seem impossible, because she gave him the example of being persistent and never failing. After the funeral João took the boy, now under his responsibility, to stay at his home and he stayed there for a few days.

But he ended up not adapting to the new stay and insisted on wanting to return home. Lucia had prepared the boy to survive without alone, she knew that something unexpected could happen to her suddenly and she trained him perfectly.

Despite his young age, he knew how to do all the chores in the house. He cooked very well, washed his clothes and was a good janitor. In agreement with John he returned home and there he lived with his new friend Pingo, a dog that he received as a gift from Mr. Bethe, a very old woman who lived next door.

It was she who kept an eye on the orphan and took care of everything while he studied in the morning and in the afternoon he worked in the market, where before the accident he worked alongside his mother. It was she who kept an eye on the orphan and took care of everything while he studied in the morning and in the afternoon he worked in the market.

Where before the accident he worked alongside his mother. Pedro's life could have been the same as many other boys his age, but unfortunately it was not so. The other boys from the neighborhood and the school made fun of him

— Look, guys, that poor devil from the slum! This wretch was abandoned by his father and now neither mother has more!

— It is a mangy dog

Lives like a dog eating the leftover that falls from the table of others —
Commented the other kids of the school where he studied

Silence was what he gave them in response to their affront. He remembered what his mother said to him while he was by his side, that we must fight back the offenses with a lot of work so that one day we will grow up and become so high that our enemies have to raise their heads to see us.

Sometimes the affront was so severe that it ended in violence, the other boys beat him up and Elisabeth, one of the girls who walked in the middle of the crowd that used to scoff at him, was the one who took the pain and went to defend him from the aggressions. She was one of the most beautiful girls in high school, but in the face of such persecution Peter did not even notice this detail in his defender.

— Wow, but because you like to oppress this poor guy, leave him alone!

— Come on, you little white girl, stop messing around where you're not being called!

— Bunch of animals, I wanted to see if he had a father to defend him if they would treat him that way

— Yeah, but it turns out he has no one, he is a dog without an owner! — Answer one of them

— Yeah, he's an orphan! — Add another

— Flock of filthy pigs, I don't know why I'm still with you! — replied the teenager, then left after helping the boy to get up

Due to being scorned by his colleagues for his financial and family condition, the boy became a reserved and lonely boy, without real friendships and intimidated by criticism, he cut himself off from everyone.

Sometimes Elisabeth tried to comfort him during recess breaks, accompanied him to his house on the outskirts and on one occasion he even met João who liked the teenager with a pale face and full of freckles, but polite and kind. Besides showing a lot of affection for the boy, which already counted a lot.

During the absence of his only friend, he had only the support of João and the inseparable friend Pingo, the dog that he received as a gift from his stepfather and who did not let go of his foot for even a minute, until he went to school he waited for him in the vicinity and followed him closely on the way home. He was the only one who seemed to understand his loneliness.

— Come Pingo, come on!

The dog did not exchange his company for anything and often listened to him very carefully, turning his muzzle and ears as if he really understood his words.

— I can't understand why people are so bad, Pingo

They hurt us just out of pure evil. Is being an orphan so terrible that they treat me with so much contempt? — the animal moved its pointy ears as if it gave him some positive confirmation answer — hell, if my father had not left, he would fix them! Ah, my little friend, even worse than now even mom left me, I'm alone for good

His conversations with the dog were constant, he knew how to vent his frustrations with the animal more than other human beings, nor did João manage to make him open up about his dissatisfactions in life. Elisabeth has been revealing to the elderly about the constant cases of mockery that the boy went through with other schoolmates and that worried him a lot.

Despite the repeated insistence that he share his concerns with his stepfather, Pedro preferred to talk to Pingo, his dog, perhaps because he remained all the time, without interfering in his many confessions. That afternoon, under a tree he once again shared his sadness with his friend.

— Mom was the best person in the world, because she always listened to me. She was just like you, Pingo, she knew how to listen and gave me advice. You know how to listen to my conversations, but you can't give me advice because you can't speak.

The wind was blowing strong and the drops of water started to fall, it was the time of the traditional three-hour rain that in the North is never late.

— Come Pingo, let's look for a place to shelter, because it will rain heavily!
— made the invitation to the dog that even if he had not been invited would have accompanied him — Let's stay here and wait for the storm!

In a few minutes the storm falls over the whole city and from the narrow window of the small deposit that the stepfather built to store tools he observed. Lucy used it frequently while she was alive, there she put her stuff. That weekend Peter and his dog used the place to shelter from the rain. He was just a boy, but he was not afraid to live alone in that place, with only the company of his animal.

On the right side lived Mrs. Maria, whose daughter sometimes came to her house to touch her sex. Since she was young, she already showed she didn't have much character and when she turned fifteen she gave it to anyone who was interested.

At the age of eleven he was an overweight type and she loved to stroke his limb that stretched like an elastic band. He did everything he wanted and hooked the kid who wanted to play every day. As he was a shy and repressed kid, the mothers around him never suspected what really happened inside the house and this greatly facilitated the pranks of the two teenagers. In this way, the neighbor's daughter was the one who initiated the sexual life of little Peter, motherless and abandoned by his father whom he never met.

In the following days, the boy continued to be disturbed by his schoolmates despite Elisabeth's many interventions, which led the little boy to be absent for several weeks from classes and the teachers decided to intervene in the situation. He missed classes, but none of the neighbors noticed.

He dressed as usual and went towards the school, but went out of the way, always going in other directions always in the company of his dog, so the neighborhood believed he was participating regularly in his studies. In the afternoon he returned and after preparing something to eat he went to the fair to help João with sales at the fruit stand. However, Elisabeth decided to interfere and that morning she went to her house and encouraged him to expose everything to her stepfather.

So they went to meet the elderly and the girl reported to the elderly what had been happening to the boy at school, requesting that some action be taken about. The next day, the elderly man went to the board of directors to report the facts to the director of the institution, who promised to notify the parents of the students in question about their children's behavior against the little orphan, as they acted in a prejudiced manner. For a time he had peace, the aggressions stopped and he was able to be treated with more dignity, though too late. Because of the difficult life and the many persecutions suffered by the other boys.

The prejudice and the lonely life the teenager started to want to look for new directions and made wrong friendships. At thirteen he mixed with bad elements that addicted him to drugs and alcohol. Despite the many attempts by those closest to him who wanted to help him, nothing stopped him.

Several times he was caught stealing nearby in the company of criminals and was taken to Institute child's house, where he received guidance from psychologists and then released as ordered by the Statute of Minors and Adolescents. By the age of fifteen, he had already become the terror of the neighborhood and the most dangerous minor offender in the entire periphery where he commanded the drug trade and a strong gang of bandits.

The old house where he lived with his mother became his headquarters and his reputation for evil has gone so far that not even the local police dared to invade his territory. However, on one occasion a delegate of the Federal Police of extreme boldness decided to face the criminal child and put an end to that disappointing situation in which the authorities found themselves until then.

— It is not possible that we, as representatives of the society that elected us to defend it, would be at the mercy of such a trickster and bow our heads in the face of its violent and threatening dictates. Therefore, I received permission from the highest command to form a task force to invade that nest of fleas and exterminate once and for all with such boldness on the part of those infamous.

I order that ten teams of twenty men each be created and arm themselves to the teeth with the best weaponry available and start the mission immediately!

— Yes ma'am! — Responded promptly one of the commanded

— I want only the best in this mission, no beginners or anyone who has no experience in the subject!

— Leave it, delegate!

Angelina Flores was a dynamic woman in her commitments as a police officer, dynamic, courageous to the fullest and her tenacity commanded respect before her subordinates and professional colleagues. That Monday morning.

As he began preparing a platoon to fight one of the most feared drug dealers in the peripheral area of the city of Belem, located in the northern region of the country, he knew that this would not be a task easy, however, her wit did not let her falter.

While the attack plan was being elaborated inside the Federal Police's premises in the capital of Pará in the favela, Pedro, now a feared drug dealer, was notified by his team of informants that he intelligently infiltrated into the various areas of police action in order to always be aware of the news against him and his criminal kingdom, he became aware of everything the authorities planned.

— ... And they intend to invade the area on Friday at dawn. While still many sleep, intending to take us by surprise

— Bunch of imbeciles, and since when do crime scouts sleep?

— They are some suckers — added one of the bandits.

— Well, thanks for the information, Leandro, now go back and continue there quietly, be sure to let us know of any change in their plans and be careful, do not come here in person, write us through the message application as we had agreed, because may be being followed

— Okay, boss, it was bad!

We'll be prepared to face that shitty delegate!

— It's not him, boss, it's her!

— How come, you're telling me that who dared to dismantle my drug trade here in the favela is a fucking pussy?

— That's right, boss!

— But what a daring of this bitch, I will have the greatest pleasure of taking this dirty bitch alive and turning her inside out until she learns to respect me!

— This is screwed! — Added another of the criminals for knowing the drug dealer's reputation for harshly punishing his opponents.

— Now let's act, guys, get all our people together and let them know what's coming.

Pass on the information to scouts throughout the lowlands and also to those active in the distribution of drugs throughout the city. Don't leave anyone unaware!

— Leave it, I'll take care of that personally — Says the manager Cristiano.

He was the traffic manager in the entire periphery and in the four corners of the city, his malice was so great that Peter put him as his right arm in charge of his criminal empire. After that conversation, all the members of the largest gang of criminals in the state were ready for any movement by the police who until that moment believed they could take them by surprise.

The Federal Police delegate, Angelina Flores, was mistaken when she thought that because she was facing a teenager she would have the ability to surprise him at home. Even at a young age, Peter became an agile crime leader after he killed the cripple, the largest and most feared drug dealer in the region whose command power covered the entire State of Pará.

His death came after a huge confrontation against the teenagers' men, who added up to twice those who protected the then commander of the drug trade, leading those left and other faction leaders to respect him and follow his orders. After being informed by the intelligence of the PF about who in fact was that boy whom he intended to confront in combat the police officer sweated cold.

And for the first time felt a chill that started in the trunk of his spine and went to the last strand of his hair. in the head. Especially when he heard, from the person who read all the criminal's file, all the details of his many crimes committed against his enemies. The most terrible was the one that led him to burn six of his opponents alive, after torturing them until they regretted the boldness of confronting him.

According to the information obtained by the intelligence of the PF, "The Red Skull", as he became known for his violent and merciless practices, would have plucked in cold blood all the nails and feet of the poor devils, using pliers.

Then he cut his ears with a knife, marked his buttocks with a red-hot iron, placing the initials "T.R.S." who made reference to their codename in the crime and finally ordered them to be tied to a wooden post, then burned them alive.

— My goodness, what human being would do that to his fellow men?

— "The Red Skull" did, lady

— This evil element needs to be stopped as soon as possible! — Added the deputy delegate

— And it will be, Ricardo, you can be sure of that! From now on this will be my highest priority as a delegate

— I would like to inform you that we are already with the teams all ready to execute the mission, we await your orders

— Perfectly, then this weekend we will invade that den of criminals as planned

— Yes, ma'am

The week seemed to go by slowly and during all the time Angelina was anxious to imagine the immense challenge that awaited her. The six men tortured and burned alive by the bandit were all Federal Police agents who infiltrated his faction in order to obtain information about their actions and pass them on to their superiors, so that in this way they could outline an invasion plan in command trafficking and arrest the criminal.

She wondered about the possibilities of succeeding in that almost impossible mission, since her opponent seemed to have unlimited power over all other drug lords across the state and the number of his men was five times greater than those of the PF. It was night and the deputy was talking to her assistant on her cell phone about the difficult task they were going to face.

— It won't be easy, Ricardo, this element is not just any bad guy

— Certainly not, Delegate, this one will be hard work

— But we, too, don't use these badges for nothing!

— I fully agree with you, we will not chicken out!

— In two days we will see who's who after the confrontation

— As I told you, all the teams are already ready

— Great, now it's just waiting for time to act

— Have we received the command's release yet?

— Yes, everything is in order

— Okay, ma'am, so we just have to wait for the time to start the action

— That's right, Ricardo, good night

— Sleep well delegated

Despite what his friend and assistant wanted, it was impossible for him to have a peaceful sleep that night in the face of such expectation. Angelina feared not only for her own life, but also for her followers.

Two hundred agents, among well-trained and armed men and women to the teeth, would accompany her on that suicide mission, she felt the chill take over her body every time she thought about it.

Second Part

The invasion

If, on the one hand, Delegate Angelina Flores lost her sleep because of the enormous challenge that would come two days ahead of her, The Red Skull hoped that moment would be shortened, because she wanted to look deep in the eyes of the one she wanted to defeat and then do with her all the evil that he dreamed of practicing with a woman, in front of all his followers.

He had already won the title of wickedness due to the atrocities practiced against his enemies, but never against a woman. His evil mind urged him to possess her in the most terrible way Violating her with the use of acts of sodomy and savagery that would make her cry out in pain and despair at the perplexed looks of those who were there. Without a doubt, what was being reserved for the fearless PF Delegate. If she lost the battle and was captured still alive, it was something never imagined by healthy minds.

The better her death would be than having to face such martyrdom at the hands of her aggressor.

— Chief, what do you think of doing if we manage to catch the doggie of the little police officer? — Interrogates Pimentinha, one of his personal security

— I'm going to roll up all the bitch holes and turn her inside out in front of all of you and the assholes of the canes who walk with the naughty and remain alive after the massacre that will be the fuck, I'll show you how to fuck a bitch wearing a uniform police!

— Fuck, this time the boss is going to fuck it!

— You have no idea what I'm planning to do with that fucking bitch!

— I know what your intention is, yes, boss, you want to put the general terror in the trickery and show who's boss!

— He spoke and said, my comrade, I want to have general power over the other commanders of the drug trade and become the dread of everyone!

— That's it, boss, the more evil you do in front of them the more they will fear and respect you!

— And is that not the idea, Pimentinha? I will dominate general!

Finally, the day of the invasion in charge of the drug trade led by Case approached. If she lost the battle and was captured still alive it was something never imagined by healthy minds.

The better her death would be than having to face such martyrdom at the hands of her aggressor.

— Chief, what do you think of doing if we manage to catch the doggie of the little police officer? — Interrogates Pimentinha, one of his personal security

— I'm going to roll up all the bitch holes and turn her inside out in front of all of you and the assholes of the canes who walk with the naughty and remain alive after the massacre that will be the fuck, I'll show you how to fuck a bitch wearing a uniform police!

— Fuck, this time the boss is going to fuck it!

— You have no idea what I'm planning to do with that fucking bitch!

— I know what your intention is, yes, boss, you want to put the general terror in the trickery and show who's boss!

— He spoke and said, my comrade, I want to have general power over the other commanders of the drug trade and become the dread of everyone!

— That's it, boss, the more evil you do in front of them the more they will fear and respect you!

— And is that not the idea, Pimentinha? I will dominate general!

Finally, the day of the invasion at the head of the drug trade led by the Red Skull and his followers was approaching, which were in great numbers. The Delegate and her agents put themselves in position.

They positioned themselves in an old warehouse located not far from the place where the confrontation with the traffickers would take place and outline an attack scheme.

— How many agents do we have for the confrontation?

— Two hundred, Delegate, as requested

— Okay, Ricardo, then we will be divided into four groups of fifty and we will attack all at once, but we will appear over the scoundrels on all sides. I will lead the group towards the North, you with the agents of the South and name those who will lead the two other groups East and West. I want to see if these scoundrels will be able to get away from this attack after being surrounded from all corners and under heavy rain of bullets

— Delegate, are you not taking into account the innocent civilians who happen to be between us and the enemies?

— And since when is there a good person in a place like that, Ricardo?

— But will you not even consider the children an exception, Delegate?

— Ricardo, in this world of trafficking even children sell drugs

— Even so, we cannot commit a slaughter against civilians without taking into account that there are innocent people among them! Look here, boy, the Delegate here is me. The PF Command gave me carte blanche to put an end to this nest of asps.

And if inside there are poisonous snakes of any age they will take lead just like any other. The order is to destroy the entire trafficking army and then burn everything, regardless of whether there will be innocent victims or not. Besides what we know there are no families there, the area is exclusive for trafficking. Therefore, if you do not agree with the measures adopted by your superiors, resign your duties right now and pass on your position to one of your subordinates more capable and able to obey!

— Sorry, ma'am, let's follow your orders

Ricardo occupied the position of voice delegate of the PF in the State of Pará and could lose his functions if he insisted on discussing the orders of his superiors, as the hierarchy should be respected. Thus, she hesitated in the face of the threats made by the Delegate and chose to comply with her orders, even though she was completely against the inhumane way in which she intended to act in an attempt to destroy the largest focus of drug trafficking in the region.

— Listen carefully to my recommendations: The main goal to be achieved in this surprise attack on the snake's nest of trafficking is to eliminate any.

And all members that are part of it. Destroy the entire supply of drugs found on the site, incinerating everything, we have no intention of holding hostages, order is death for all these bastards! When confronting enemies, shoot to kill without pain or pity, this is an order and must be carried out, understand?

— Yes ma'am!!! — All repeated unanimously

It was still dawn that Friday, when the four groups of federal agents headed towards the lowlands where the central crime office led by the region's biggest drug dealer was located. Commonly known as "The Red Skull", feared for its ferocity and malice towards his opponents.

Those involved in the hasty mission were divided into four teams and boldly advanced towards what would be a true suicide. Delegate Angelina led one of the groups of fifty agents and her deputy with two other experienced companions commanded the remaining troops.

The attack on the traffickers took place before dawn when they were supposed to be less attentive to a possible assault by the police, however, to the surprise of the feds all of them were awake and attentive to their opponents' invasion plan which resulted in an unexpected reaction.

Dangerous for each of the members of the first two groups that entered the territory of the crime who were received under a strong volley of large-caliber bullets.

Leading the majority to death in a matter of seconds, this has already resulted in a vast disarticulation on the part of the invaders. Who retreated in frightened by the unexpected reaction of the enemies, since they believed they could take them by surprise. When realizing that the teams that acted in the east and west direction of the trafficking territory failed.

Angelina and Ricardo decided to take a risk in a new attack which led the bandits to react with greater firepower against them. The delegate and her agents found themselves under a powerful firestorm from all over whose parts their weapons possessed an unprecedented capacity for destruction, causing their men to fall with immense ease in front of their opponents.

Ricardo makes the decision to order the immediate retreat of his men to prevent further deaths, however, Angelina insisted on staying on the battlefield and this cost her all her followers the death, she was soon overpowered and became a prisoner of the terrible drug dealer. In the distance the colleague of the profession, together with the few who remained of his team, watched the situation unfold without being able to intervene.

The bold Federal Delegate was taken to the presence of the leader of the drug trade and thrown by those who led her to her feet in an act of humiliation and shame for the authorities who were in charge of putting an end to their empire.

Once again he emerged victorious before his opponents. Fallen at the criminal's feet after being slapped by his men, Angelina still breathed airs of power and threatened him with punishment, showing that she was convinced that her superiors would not let that affront cheaply. She still breathed airs of power and threatened him with punishment.

Showing that she was fully convinced that her superiors would not let that affront cheaply.

— Damn you, do you have any idea what will happen after you kill all those federal agents?" The highest summits of authorities in this country will fall on you and your lackeys without the least pity!

The criminal places his right foot on the prisoner's back and makes her kiss the dust on the floor where she was in a shameful position and warns her with irony:

— But what idiocy to think that those corrupt are concerned with saving your skin and these poor devils who sent to die in my territory, my delegate, your superiors will not care for the result of this operation and if you have fallen from grace they will close their eyes and let the worst happen to you!

He lifts her off the floor and threatens her face to face, looking deep into her eyes.

— Now come with Daddy.

You little cow, who will show you what I do with anyone who dares to challenge me!

— Miserable, you will pay dearly for all this! - She kicks in vain

He drags her by holding her hair towards a point where it would be possible to give him the punishment he thought was the most convenient. He fulfilled what he had promised his men initially.

And when he arrived at his destination, the monstrous bandit ordered his group to form a large circle around him and the Delegate, then proceeded to undress her in the presence of those present who mocked her humiliating situation.

— Well done you bitch! - Some spoke

— Shameless dog! - exclaimed others

While they laughed and criticized her martyrdom, the criminal took off her clothes and left her completely undressed, despite her many efforts to try to prevent rape.

— Be quiet, you bitchy bitch!

— Go to hell, you bastard monster!

He throws her down on the floor totally naked and throws himself between her legs.

Which were kept open by two of the spectators, because they were muscular, it was immensely difficult for the young man to keep them in that position and still group her.

— That's it, boss, fuck this fucking bitch!

— Splinter the stick in that pan!

With no way of avoiding rape, she is finally violently penetrated by the voracious enemy who stuck her giant mast in it until it hit the cable. After much punching in all his holes in an animalistic way.

Practicing anal sex with such savagery that it tore his anus to the point of bleeding, causing him to scream in terrible pain, still in complete desperation he forced him to open his mouth and I swallowed his endowed penis in size and thickness, punching it in the throat to the sac.

Throughout the show Ricardo and his companions who survived the confrontation with the miscreants accompanied him from afar without being able to do anything to free her from that monstrous situation. They remained hidden in a thicket near the place, on the banks of the Utinga River, which was an environmental reserve area used by the city for the city's water supply.

After using and abusing the victim who was at the mercy of the bandits and was painfully tortured by them, "The Red Skull" handed her over to his cronies who began to abuse the poor thing.

At least about twenty males also raped her, shoving their big and small penises, thick or thin, into her fleshy ass and vagina, as well as punching at her already sore throat at will.

That day Angelina saw the doors of hell open for her and wished for them to pass without ever having to return just to free herself from such pain and shame, because she had never been so humiliated before. After that macabre scene, the insensitive drug dealer ordered her to be dragged to one of the several shacks in the immediate vicinity.

And give him a bath to improve his appearance, because due to the mistreatment he was in a deplorable state.

— Clean that filthy bitch and then take her to my sector!

— Leave it, boss! Come on, you fucking bitch!

They took her to a place where there was a jet washing machine and after being positioned in any corner of the room, she was thrown with strong bursts of water so that the dirt could be removed from her body. Then they took her back to the presence of the leader who waited impatiently.

— Fuck, at last!

— Calm down, boss, this stink was a job!

— Okay, leave her here with me and get out!

After being rolled on the floor of the old wooden house again.

He raises his face towards her eyes and disdains her humiliating situation.

— And now, fierce delegate, what is your next threat after being fucked by me and my men until you bleed that bitch's ass?

She takes advantage of the criminal's carelessness and boldly slaps his face, being matched accordingly. He grabs her hair and starts to slap her across the face, punches and kicks all over her body until she collapses. Then he throws a portion of cold water over his head to wake him up again.

— Come on, bitch, wake up!

She wakes up stunned and leans back in an old, moldy armchair that existed in the mold-covered place, giving the distinct feeling of not being used or properly cleaned for a long time. The maniac lays her on the floor of the shack and takes advantage of her nakedness to invade her body again in the fulfillment of her wild desires.

After licking the inside of her vagina, sucking on her clit and sucking on her fleshy breasts, he shoves her powerful member into that fleshy and luscious pussy, strongly leveraging strong back and forth movements that made her moan in pain and not in pleasure. As he had promised his lackeys, he would perform on his adversary the worst acts of sexual savagery that he had kept in mind since he was molested by the daughter of the neighbor who molested him when he was a child and taught him all the immoralities he never forgot.

Tired of penetrating it just from the front, he took her by the long hair and forced her to lie on all fours, putting the giant mast in her tight little hole without punishment until it hit the trunk and at that moment she gave another strong moan and cried.

Despite being raped by several men at the same time and being beaten several times in the course of the martyrdom, still resisted. She endured the suffering caused by the merciless bandit.

Could still feel her anus being torn once more, perhaps because he was the biggest and thickest of all the others. Satisfied with everything he had practiced with the woman, he allowed her to rest from torture and she remained right there on the coarse wooden floor for several hours, without eating or drinking.

Until she woke up, she was taken to another place to be cared for by the women who served the king of the trade in order to give him clothes and heal their wounds. All of this happened in a period of at least ten hours and during that time Ricardo and his followers only waited for the end of the outcome to be completely impotent, however inconsolable for being unable to do anything.

— I can't conform, until when will we have to stay in that inertia without being able to help her?

— I don't know, maybe even the cavalry will help us

— What cavalry are you talking about, Leandro, do you happen to dream of the possibility that any of those damned bureaucrats remember that we are in the middle of this hell?

— But of course, after all they were the ones who sent us here!

— Don't be naive, boy, the Delegate was solely responsible for this suicide mission and for putting us in this dead end.

The High Command only accepted her request because she is the daughter of a retired general. Who knows if they still believe there are survivors

— Daughter of a bitch! So, being like this we are really in trouble

— You bet

— And you are still there worried about her?

— It is my duty, we are partners and one should not abandon a companion in a battle, whatever it may be

— Know. And learned all this bullshit of fidelity to the combat partner where, in the Armed Forces?

— No, with life ... Attention, Freitas, do you still have your cell phone?

— Yes, and working!

— Try to contact someone from the Command and see if you can ask for reinforcements, inform them of our situation and the correct location. Explain the failure of the operation and warn about the capture of the Delegate!

— Leave it to me!

Ricardo abruptly ended the dialogue with Leandro without realizing that he was an informant for the "Red Skull", infiltrated the PF in order to let him know about all the strategies made against his territory. While the deputy delegate struggled with his team to request reinforcements. So they did this together with the Federal Police High Command, but not too far from there, the criminals planned to pay the authorities back for daring to challenge them.

— So, boss, are we just going to be defensive or are we going to go over the guys?

— Are you wondering, Formiga, since when do I have to be alone in the boom after someone decides to face me? Of course we are going to bring down the terror on these bastards!

— That's it, boss, and how's the parade going to be? — adds Azulão, one of the flock

— Wait a minute I'll think

— We have to know how to stop - warns another

— Now you want to teach the boss how to set up the plans, bro?

Fixes a criminal room

— Do you want to stop making waves? The boss is fucking thinking! —

Alert Cristiano who was the right arm of Skull

After much analysis of the pros and cons of the situation, the head of drug trafficking decides to immediately gather all his cronies who worked in drug trafficking in the capital and sent a message through a messaging app, summoning them to be present that afternoon.

At first, he heard a certain fear of other drug trafficking leaders coming to the meeting, as they feared being taken by surprise by the reinforcements that would certainly be sent by the authorities after learning about the death of the feds last night, when they attempted a frustrated attack against The Red Skull And his band, however, after the strong threats made by him decided to obey his orders and all were present, as determined by the biggest and most fearful of all the traffickers.

— Good that everyone came, because the matter is urgent. Those sons of a PF whore decided to face us early and took the bran and now we have to give change to the bastards

— And you want to count on us in this?

— No, I'm calling everyone to join this one, could you get the deal? Here I don't ask anyone for anything, damn it, I tell them to do it and obey it!

At the same moment that he exalts himself, his subordinates cock their weapons in an attack position to those who might refuse to disobey their greatest commander and they chicken out.

— Calm down, let's talk - Intercede one of them

— I'm in the conversation, you guys who turned yellow!

— Come on, explain the plan - Requested another

— It's very simple, let's get down on those bastards!

— Okay, but where do we start?

— Fuck, am I speaking Greek to you, you kids? I already said that we're going to put our finger on those bastards of PF! Organize groups of as many men as you can and have them terrorized. They can kill, kidnap and even burn their house, do whatever it takes for those fuckers to respect us, show them who's boss in this fucking city!

The rest of the crime leaders no longer wanted to challenge the orders of the most fearful of all criminals and promised to act immediately, fearing that their anger would turn against themselves. From afar, still stuck in the nearby forest, Ricardo and the other agents watched the movement in the drug trafficking office and saw when several large crime fish arrived and immediately afterwards they left in their imported cars, concluding that it was a meeting between the big bosses to put some plan into action.

— Sons of a mare, they certainly plan to pay the Command back for the boldness we had to confront them

— Is that really possible, Ricardo?

After all, we are talking about the highest echelon of the PF — One of the

agents

— Can you believe so, my friend, did you happen to see what that bastard

did to our Delegate and how he wiped out the other agents? The power of

influence of the traffic over the great ones of that country is unlimited.

Você pode ter certeza de que eles buscarão o apoio de todos aqueles que

lhes devem favor, sejam eles os mais altos escalões da sociedade, políticos e

autoridades ainda mais altas, para que cheguem o mais próximo possível de

seus descontentes e então o terror desça sobre eles

—Oh my God!

— I'm even sorry for them

— And the Delegate, Ricardo, is she still alive or did these bastards kill her

as they did with the other agents?

— No, they should know that she is not an ordinary agent like the others

and will know how to value her importance

— It's true, Deputy Angelina is the daughter of a big fish from the reserve

and what they did to her won't be cheap

— Of that I'm sure, however, they will demand a high value for her life if

the reinforcements that come in order to rescue her end up like us, dead or

imprisoned in this hell

— Believe me, Ricardo

The two agents exchanged opinions while awaiting the arrival of reinforcements, hidden in the forest of the environmental reserve, after having already informed their superiors about the failure of the mission, the dozens of deaths of the other agents and the capture of the delegate.

And, during that time, the bandits devised all the necessary strategy to bring terror to the big Federal Police, both in the capital and throughout the state. Mafiosi communicated via social networks, phone calls, messaging apps and even by video conference with those who were more distant and were unable to attend in person at meetings held at various points of action of the various factions that joined forces in order to avenge the invasion to the territory of the fearsome "Red Skull".

Trapped in one of the drug trafficking hiding places, Angelina was watched day and night by the drug lord's men, who occasionally passed by and owned her at will. Transformed into a sex slave to her worst enemy, she didn't even care about her health.

If she would be pregnant with the monster that continually raped her without the care to use a condom or if she had contracted some malignant disease, because of so much suffering she no longer had the hope of leaving there alive.

Locked in a dark room, tied to a fetid and moldy bed, she kept her eyes closed while allowing herself to fly in her thoughts for the old life she had before entering that endless well. Her memories led her to a beautiful and peaceful childhood with her family, until her mother's death at the hands of a criminal.

Lieutenant Colonel and PF Chief Evandro de Almeida Flores was, at the time, the commander of a secret investigation against corrupt politicians belonging to various parties who were involved in the embezzlement of public money.

Deputies, senators and a wide range of businessmen and civil servants would be involved in a millionaire scheme that economically sank the country and led millions of Brazilian workers to unemployment and others to total misery.

Due to his insistence on presenting positive results in his investigations, he ended up irritating some of the most violent who decided to take his life, which happened when he returned from his farm located in the south of the state. Being shot by them by several shots. However, who lost his life was his wife after the two spent several days on the verge of death in an ICU. The murder of her mother at the behest of her father's enemies, led the young Angelina Flores to wish to join the Federal Police.

To fight corruption among the leaders of her country and prevent impunity from reigning over those who practiced everything and paid nothing for the crimes committed. against a society completely helpless by those who should protect it. In this way, she prepared herself properly and after completing the Criminal Law course she was approved as a Federal Delegate.

With her training and the help of her father, she entered the desired role and had several successes in the missions entrusted to her until that day, when she seemed to have been abandoned by luck.

Known for her perspicacity and never retreating in the face of danger, she overcame all perspectives and won the admiration and respect of her professional colleagues, led, superiors and the father who always supported her a lot in the career she embraced.

Since his capture by the criminals, the then colonel of the reserve Evandro Flores had no more peace and was bitter about his daughter's disappearance. Her pain increased even more after she learned of the condition in which she was being tortured and abused by the bandits. Its enormous influence has led several authorities to organize a Task Force made up of dozens of agents and hundreds of military personnel, also counting on duly armed army men with the mission of rescuing it from the hands of the terrible criminals.

But the slowness in implementing the plan drawn up by the teams involved resulted in the counterattack of the traffickers on those who ordered the invasion of the territory of the traffic headed by The Red Skull.

Impotent to free his partner from the enemy, with only a few men, Ricardo decides to leave the territory of the drug trade and return to the capital together with his companions.

The rescue of the agents took place by car on a highway at least a kilometer away from where they were previously. Arriving at the PF he reported everything to his superiors who promised to intervene and rescue the delegate as soon as possible.

Third Part

The Rematch

The invasion of the main Federal Police agency in the capital by a gang composed of more than twenty duly armed men that resulted in the kidnapping of those responsible for the direction of the sectors destined to combat the narcotics and narcotics trafficking.

As well as the general directorship of that body. federal government and in the death of several agents who tried to prevent the action of the miscreants, the biggest carnage that has never been seen until today in the Northern Region of Brazil began.

Everything happened in a few minutes and the success of the criminal operation was because Leandro, the bandit infiltrated in the PF at the behest of Red Skull, facilitated the location of the victims within the agency and provided accurate data of how many agents would be present at the time of the invasion. Ten federal police officers died in the confrontation.

And their directors were forcibly driven to the crime territory under the command of the drug dealer. The number of people kidnapped by the bandits was four, each leading an important sector to fight organized crime in the State of Pará and when the Secretary of Public Security was notified of the incident, along with the other competent authorities, they immediately informed the Governor that with they met to plot a rescue plan for the victims.

However, while discussing what would be the best strategy to be used in this case, the criminals continued to terrorize the lives of those they considered to be responsible for the bold attack on the headquarters of the traffic located in one of the peripheries of the city of Belem.

After torturing the four men who were victimized by the "Red Skull" kidnapping and their men, they obtained the exact location of their homes and soon sent dozens of bandits to invade these places, steal everything of value from there and lower the terror in their homes. relatives.

The order given by chief number one of the traffic was to destroy what was of no use in those places, to beat, to torture whoever was there and to take their children to captivity together with their wives. The invasion of the houses took place during the early hours of the day and when they realized what had happened, the military and civil police could do nothing.

In each of the residences, about ten men were present, who eliminated the security guards, using weapons with silencers to muffle the sound of bullets, defusing alarms and entering the environment without being noticed by those who met there. Their desperation when they realized that the property had been invaded by criminals was indescribable, however, the surrender was inevitable when they realized the gravity of the situation.

Before the prisoners were taken to the territory of the crime, the miscreants tied the adults up and raped the younger girls in their presence, then slapped the older ones in the sight of their children and grandchildren. The barbarity of the bandits was unlimited and they carried out to the letter the orders given by the main commander of the crime.

Then they took all the prisoners into captivity and met there with the rest of them. Dissatisfied with only kidnapping the Federal Police directors in the capital, The Red Skull ordered that they also be brought in to join those who already had other Public Security leaders as a hostage to their power.

While the investigations followed the criminals' tracks, they moved in another direction in an attempt to implement new actions, always one step ahead of investigators and weak military intelligence. The Governor and his advisors continued their long meetings. They almost always left the room dissatisfied with the results of their conclusions.

And seemed to have their hands tied in the face of the wave of violence that criminals spread day after day in the city and the Public Security Secretariat had its leader replaced, since the previous one did not respond. immediate control of the chaos in which society succumbed.

After having in his power all the most important representatives of the Public Security of the State Red Skull decided to act with more violence on the victims in order to show the immensity of his empire and of who was the last word in that place, thus, he passed to torture them while with a camera one of his followers filmed everything.

— Bring those rascals, their sons, daughters and women here to the salon!

— Yes, boss!

Everyone gathered in the spacious hall of the shed built to hold their usual parties and the torture began.

— I want to see all these tasty naked in front of me!

As the young women and some adolescents did not comply with the trafficker's request, she immediately lacked patience.

— Now, damn it, take off your fucking clothes or I'll kill your parents! - Threatened him with gun in hand

— Come on, you bitches, the boss was serious! — Commented Formiga quite puzzled by the situation

The eight girls began to undress in the presence of the bandit and at the look of despair of their family members who could do nothing to protect them. Then they are sexually abused by the perpetrators who once again raped them and forced them to practice all kinds of sex in front of their parents and siblings who only responded to the violence with screams and tears.

Still dissatisfied with such barbarism, they also began to rape the wives of the police and forced them to watch everything with their eyes wide open so that they would not be shot in the center of the forehead, the women were forced to undress in front of their spouses, children and daughters.

And then suck the member of several of his assailants and swallowed their cock until it hit the sack. When they threatened to provoke vomiting, they were hit hard on the face and thus swallowed everything without dirtying the penis of those who raped it.

They were put on all fours with their white asses tucked in the direction of their companions and then stuck in their two holes by thick limbs until nothing was left out, some who never seemed to have had anal sex screamed like bitches when they were ripped open. The males did not want to see those scenes of complete violence, but they were compelled to do so, as they remained in the crosshairs of other thugs. Who received the ordinance to put a bullet in them if they closed their eyes.

Never have those rich women fucked so much in life or been punched by so many cocks. The sequence of animal acts continued without time to end and the bandits took advantage of the heat of sexual cannibalism to drink alcohol, smoke marijuana, smell various types of dust and have fun at the expense of their victims' misfortune. On the other hand, the Government, together with its advisors, secretaries and various authorities, continued to try to find a way to invade the place where PF directors and their families were held in captivity without putting them at risk.

— Tell me, gentlemen, how will we manage to dismantle that nest of poisonous snakes without endangering our people who remain captive by criminals?

— Mister Governor, it is almost impossible to imagine a way to free the hostages from putting them at risk - Advances the Secretary of Security

— But then, what will we do in face of this, will we sit idly by without taking any action to solve the problem or will we continue here, wasting time, with this conversation that always results in nothing?

— You are absolutely right, but we have not yet found any method that would allow us to act without the victims being in any danger.

— And the Colonels and other authorities present here also fail to give us an idea that can leverage this indecision?

O Caveira Vermelha - Romance

— In fact the only way to invade that captivity is to endanger the lives of the kidnapped people — Answers one of them

— Mister Governor, I ask you for the opportunity to propose something that may help to resolve this issue — Proposes one of the authorities present there

— Very well, we are all ears

— As far as I was informed, the daughter of Colonel of the Reserve Evandro Flores, delegate Angelina Flores, is one of those who is incarcerated in that den of criminals of the worst kind. So, aware that he would be willing to accept any offer to free her and the vast experience he has in this field, we could call on him to join us and present the best strategy to invade the place without much casualties in our troops or endangering the lives of victims

— Of course, how had we thought about this possibility before? After all, he was considered one of the greatest organizers of hostage rescues during his time in the PF - He praised one of the Commanders of the Military Police

— Very well, then if no one in this room does not object, we will call you to join us at the next meeting that will take place tomorrow morning.

With all of them in full agreement, the summons was sent. To the retired Colonel with the official signature of the major head of the State and the following morning he was already present at the meeting.

— Thank you.

67

We appreciate your readiness to collaborate with us in making this difficult decision, Colonel

— I feel grateful for the invitation, Governor, after all my daughter is trapped in that captivity, despite having asked for help from the Civil and Military Police Command, nothing has yet been done to free her

— We understand your frustration, dear colleague, but as you can see we met without finding a way out of this dilemma — said one of those present

— In fact, Colonel, and that is exactly why we invited you to participate in this meeting with us, as we are aware of your vast experience as an articulator of plans for the release of hostages in captivity.

— And what is the greatest difficulty you have encountered in carrying out this mission, Excellency?

— We do not want to endanger the lives of the hostages at the time of the invasion by our troops, when the firearm firing starts

— Yes, of course, it would be useless to fight the enemy and as a result we lose our people without taking the hostages away alive

— Then tell us, Colonel:

What would be the best strategy to solve this situation without much casualties for our men and rescue the victims without being injured?

— I propose the following:

That we first take the hostages out of captivity and only then attack our enemies

— And how do we do that? Asked an authority puzzled

— I believe that the commanders present here have some of their Military Intelligence personnel infiltrated in various gangs scattered throughout the state and from them receive the necessary information to put into practice their schemes to fight organized crime, right? That way we will locate one of these infiltrators who may be inside or very close to the crime office headed by the "Red Skull" and in this way we will put the hostage escape plan in progress

— Very well, because it will be done! — the Governor rejoiced — Colonel you will command the entire rescue process and from that moment on, no decision can be taken in this case without your full knowledge

— Thank you, Your Excellency

Unfortunately for the authorities, Red Skull asked other factions to send reinforcements to carry out their future plans for mass destruction through the streets of the most important cities in the state. This allowed the infiltrators to be taken with extreme ease to lodge in the middle of the gang that still enjoyed themselves at the expense of the women of their prisoners. which has been happening for several days in a row. There were five agents who lived among the factions and who entered the crime office.

For a whole week they were busy acting as scouts of the crime and at the same time trying to identify the exact location where the hostages were to put their rescue plan into practice. Days after locating the captivity and informing the authorities in detail about how it would be more correct to get to the house, in addition to pointing out with cell phone images all the paths and alleys that led to the point in question, the start is made to remove the victims from that hole .

Fortunately it seemed that God or destiny were in full agreement to free them from the devil's hands and on the day that the infiltrators were given the order to begin the process of escape together with the hostages, "The Red Skull" ordered some of his lackeys to take Delegate Angelina to be with the others in the shack from which the infiltrators later planned to provide them with escape.

The next morning the vile drug dealer intended to cause the biggest uproar in the city center, along with the support of its more than two hundred men and the help of other factions.

It would be extremely necessary for the hostages to be taken out of captivity as soon as possible, as soon as squads of civilian and military police. Just as a hundred federal agents would break into the crime office and put an end to the power of their leader.

70

O Caveira Vermelha - Romance

Fifteen men guarded the site, among them the five infiltrators, which would not be difficult for the invaders to succeed in the action that would be led by Colonel Evandro Flores, who would provide battalions with radio frequency attack guidelines.

It was after midnight, when the five infiltrators wiped out the other ten miscreants, making use of methods that did not cause noise so as not to attract the attention of the other criminals, and freed the hostages, leading them on a deserted path at that moment, since they had already become familiar with the place and knew where to go.

After reaching a more distant point, they came across a vehicle that would take them to the headquarters of the Federal Police, where they would receive proper care. The infiltrators successfully complete the first part of the mission and return to their place of origin, however, they protect themselves from being an easy target during the troops' attack that would take place shortly afterwards.

Received the information that the hostages were already released from captivity, the Command gave the green light to start the invasion, however, they did not count that one of their agents was a spy. The phone rings and The Red Skull is awakened from his sleep to receive a news. That has shaken his momentary tranquility.

And he gives a shout of order to the commandos that activate the siren that served as an alert to all the miscreants in case of invasion.

— Hurry, everyone on alert, because we are being attacked! — warns Formiga — Heavy weapons against these scoundrels!

Within minutes, a violent war broke out between the criminal faction and the troops sent by the highest Command, made up of civilian and military police, in addition to federal agents. Rifle bullets, machine guns and even grenades were fired from both sides without any concern for the damage they might cause.

The crime office was located in an exclusive neighborhood for drug trafficking and there were no families or good people there, it was a type of headquarters where large quantities of different types of drugs were distributed to other factions spread across the state. In a short time of battle, dozens of combatants rolled on the ground, both on one side and on the other, however, the number of deaths was greater for the criminals who were almost surprised by the troops, which only did not happen due to the warning of Leandro who acted as an informant within the PF.

The sun was already rising, when dozens of bodies could be seen on the ground. And to further complicate the life of the bandits, more men were sent to the battlefield.

And two helicopters that began to detonate the entire territory inhabited by criminals who, contrary to what the authorities thought, responded by using a weapon of use. exclusive to the army, one of the miscreants hits one of the aircraft that explodes still in the air and its crew members turn to ashes.

Upon seeing their companions being shot down, the second aircraft withdraws from the airspace because its components understand that they would be the next to be detonated if they insisted on staying over the place. However, overland the fight would still be fought until one side was completely won.

That second attack was much more elaborate than the previous one, where the Delegate in the company of only two hundred men dared to challenge the king of the traffic, when she was defeated, lost most of her men and ended up becoming a sex slave. of the "Red Skull".

Of course, now the authorities had the vast experience of Evandro Flores and his dedication to cooperating for everything went perfectly well if he wanted to rescue Angelina and make sure that she or any other agent would never again fall victim to those murderers.

His thirst for avenging his daughter's martyrdom was limitless. Upon realizing that the Delegate and the rest of the captives had escaped The Red Skull, she was very angry.

73

And ordered that those who had been assigned to watch the place where the victims were were brought to her presence and beheaded them with her own hands, use of a long third and so sharp that it seemed to cut the wind itself. He did this to set an example for others who watched everything.

Evandro Flores was a renowned battle strategist, but despite all his experience and his military strategies being in fact the best he was unable to understand that the enemy he was dealing with was not just a teenager, now at eighteen years of age, but a cold, ruthless, determined criminal who would not easily accept defeat without fighting until the end.

In this way, his plans to destroy the crime barracks and if possible to capture the most fearful drug dealer in the state still alive was about to be frustrated, because when the troops that attacked him thought they were in a great advantage, a real army of bandits suddenly appeared who came in defense of the criminal and his gang.

There were more than three hundred men, all of them properly armed, who arrived immediately shooting at the police and in a few minutes it was possible to see the size of the troops sent to destroy the power of the traffic in that place reduced. And the commanders who led them decided to retreat, shamefully accepting that unexpected defeat. Already distant from there they informed the Command about what had happened.

And about the vast number of men who lost their lives in combat, announcing that it was inevitable to retreat before the enemies who were in greater numbers and became more powerful because their weapons were superior. Upon receiving the news, Evandro Flores was very angry and cursed his opponents.

— Damn those bastards! But how could we be surprised that way, when we already seemed to be dominating the situation and about to destroy that serpent lair?

— Sorry, Colonel, but the troops were surprised by the criminals who went there to act as reinforcements in defense of the "Red Skull" and his men

— And the new troops sent to support those already in combat, did not arrive in time to avoid this shameful retreat?

— Unfortunately yes, but it turns out that the enemies were in greater numbers than our troops

— What a disgrace! So many lives lost in vain in that fight that we already had as a win

Someone enters the office with urgent information.

— Sir, the Governor on the phone!

— Hell, there is more trouble!

The two authorities talk for a while.

And at the end of the conversation the irritated Colonel taps the phone visibly even more bored

— Warn that I need to go to a meeting urgently, prepare transport and garrison!

— Yes sir! — Someone immediately obeys the order given

The meeting took place at the Governor's Official Residence, which met there with his advisers and other senior officials, including the one responsible for the attack on the territory of the crime.

— Apparently not even all your vast experience was able to prevent many of our men from being killed in combat without, however, obtaining the desired results, Colonel?

— I must admit that you are absolutely right, Governor

— Well, at least we saved the hostages from captivity — added one of those present

— Yes, that way not everything was completely in vain — Agreed another

— Yes, gentlemen, I agree with your remarks. However, lives were lost, much blood was spilled from both sides. And in the end that damn drug dealer is still out there and right now celebrates our defeat

— Certainly, Mr. Governor - One of the authorities agrees

— And now, what will we do to recover the dignity of our troops?

And avenge those who perished in combat? Are we back to square one and doing nothing to defend the honor of our corporations?

— Yes, we will, Governor. We will outline a new attack strategy

— Sending new troops to that den of vipers is suicide! — Admits the Secretary of Security

— What we can't do is retreat under the table scared like a bunch of miserable rats! — Corrects colleague Evandro Flores

— Gentlemen, gentlemen, let's focus on what is most urgent right now. Flores, you will have your second chance against those jackals, after all there is a personal matter to be resolved between the two of you

— Certainly, he humiliated my daughter in front of all his men and abused her for several days and it will not come cheap for any of them

— And speaking of this, how is the Delegate doing?

— Recovering from the many aggressions suffered in that hell

— We are in solidarity with her and the other women who in a way were martyred by that miserable man — The other authorities present also reaffirmed the politician's words

— Thank you all — thanked the father on behalf of the daughter

— But come on, get to work, because we can't waste any more time. Right now that vulture from hell must be working on his rematch.

We can't be taken by surprise. Let's take action against your affronts and put an end to this endless war once and for all!

— We will start acting immediately, sir!

The highest representative of the State Executive Branch had no idea that his predictions would come true, because at that very moment The Red Skull also met with the other drug lords and created a plan to pay back to those who once dared to challenge him.

But, contrary to the previous act of revenge, he would not go against the authorities, but against the society that they hoped, even without any public manifestation, that the territory of the crime would be completely extinct.

In the early hours of the morning, after the sun showed its first rays, a crowd of criminals, armed to the teeth, invaded the streets of the capital of Pará, destroying everything they found in front of them.

They broke cars, shop windows, looted goods, beat anyone who dared to drive on the sidewalks and killed innocent people just to spread terror in the frightened population trying to find refuge at the first door they found open.

As soon as the crackdown began in the city, civilian and military authorities were informed. So they went out to find the wrongdoers who spread fear in people who were surprised by this violence. The confrontation took place and the population tried to protect themselves.

While the authorities fought the invaders through the streets and avenues, other groups from everywhere invaded houses, stole belongings, beat men, women and children, raped everyone they wanted, burned vehicles, plundered public assets and mocked those who held positions. of authority.

With chaos installed throughout the metropolis of Pará and realizing that the civil and military police were insufficient to prevent the spread of violence and society remained increasingly at the mercy of the bandits who spread panic and terror, the Governor declared a state of calamity public and asked the Minister of Justice for help in the Federal Capital and the next morning a plane filled with National Guard soldiers arrived.

They came to help fight crime in the city. However, twenty-four hours after the wave of destruction began in Belem, the damage was enormous, as many good citizens had their vehicles, houses, shops and various types of heritage destroyed or stolen by the factions that left the peripheries and they spread terror in the four corners of the capital that lasted for a long twenty-four hours.

The next morning, vandalism continued and the population remained trapped inside their homes, fearing that as they left the streets, they would be attacked by the cruel killers, while they continued to create general panic. The National Force fought the vandals fiercely together with the civilian and military police until finally they succeeded.

The criminals retreated and gradually were defeated. At the end of the battle the balance of bodies on the ground was large and the debris formed by vehicles and homes destroyed countless. At least for a long period, criminals would certainly not attack the population again or face their defenses in the open, because with the support received, Public Security has strengthened itself to the point of expelling them from the streets. While the city was responsible for cleaning up the mess left by the bandits the Governor in partnership with all other representatives of society and security agencies

Everyone was looking for a way to completely destroy the empire of crime.

- Gentlemen, we need to find a way to extinguish this cursed kingdom formed by these traffickers, put an end to the territory of crime as soon as possible in order to bring peace to the people of our state again

— We fully agree with you, Governor! — The mayor spoke

— That way we will have to create a new plan of attack against that den of vipers as soon as possible and it is best to be in up to forty-eight hours so that we can still catch them weak in their defenses.

— And what do you suggest we do? — Again asks the city administrator

— For this reason, the highest authorities of that State are gathered here. I want to hear the opinion of each one of you. And the proposals that allow us to send new troops for another invasion

— Colonels, what is your point of view?

— I believe that the best form of action against those criminals is the surprise attack, because they will not even have time for a reaction that leads them to have advantages over our men. Right now they are tired after the battle that took place on the streets and they do not even imagine that we will fight back in such a short time. In my opinion, we should take advantage of the support we have from the National Force and invade that nest of snakes immediately — Evandro Flores proposed.

With the full support of the other representatives of the people and the other authorities involved Evandro received carte blanche from the Governor to reorganize new troops and set off as soon as possible in a new attack against The Red Skull and his crime empire. This time with greater war power and a very expressive number of men.

With the federal order, the Brazilian army also joined the fight against traffickers, which, together with the agents and police, was a crowd. The criminal empire's bandits were outnumbered, and after their last casualty, it was still not possible to fully strengthen the factions that had joined the powerful drug dealer, so an attack at that time would be a total disaster for them. As Colonel Evandro had predicted, the troops sent caught the rascals unprepared and when they invaded the place.

They shot at their opponents surprised by the unexpected invasion, seeing them fall to the ground like dead flies. The army and the other policemen used machine guns, modern and powerful rifles, grenades and various other types of weaponry. Heavy artillery was used against enemies.

They barely responded to the attack without any positive effect. Two hours after the start of the battle, what remained was only the destruction of the site and dozens of bodies of criminals spread across the entire territory of the crime, but it was not possible to identify among the dead the slightest sign of the dealer and his closest allies. arrived, like Cristiano and Formiga who helped him in the command of the traffic.

At that time, the three had escaped and would certainly hide in one of the many slums that existed in the city and it would not be easy to locate them without the help of informants. So the way was to contact them.

Red Skull and his cronies in crime took refuge with the monkey ring, considered the second largest and most dangerous faction of the State, linked to the Red Command, led by Ronaldo Nine Fingers due to having lost one of them to being tortured by other miscreants in the past , being totally faithful to the bandit who lost his criminal empire and needed to seek refuge there. In the meantime, the authorities sought news from their informants that would lead to their capture.

The person in charge of the criminal faction advised the young drug dealer about possible flaws in his former gang.

— I do not doubt your leadership skills, but I believe that you trusted too much those who worked with you and it was certainly these who released the hostages and facilitated the first attack on your territory

— Do you believe there were police informants within my faction?

— If not, how else would the hostages escape from captivity? I believe they were placed there during the reinforcement that they asked the other factions

— So we need to be careful. What if there are police males watching us here too?

— We are not taking that risk here, my friend, because we are careful to ascertain the condition of each new member. We give the rascals a fine-tooth comb before accepting them in our midst. But certainly in the others there are many snitch

— Hell! So I really hesitated

— You bet

But, sad about this plague that dared to betray me, that shit is already dead, because as soon as I put my hands on it I will behead his head!

— Our Lady, I even felt sorry for the rascal!

— This is how I treat hard fingers

— Nothing more certain, buddy, that kind of betrayal must be crushed alive

— So you really believe that here we are free of these snitch

— This type of mouse is not created here, partner

— Okay so

What Nine Fingers had no idea was that exactly his most trusted man, apparently faithful and who never left him for a minute, was a traitor. After hearing from his boss all the conversation, he took advantage of a moment when he went to fulfill one of his personal needs and sent an alert via SMS to an individual PF contact with the information that the wanted criminals were refugees there.

As soon as the agents received the information, they passed the details to their superiors, who devised a plan to attack the place in order to arrest the three gangsters.

However, they planned not to interfere directly in the faction, as Ronaldo Nine Fingers was a well-known drug dealer, with great influences between state authorities and politicians who gained a lot from his services.

In fact, the representatives of the most corrupt people exchanged favors with the bandit and received bribes in order to give him the freedom to market his drugs throughout the region from police interference. Therefore, the order given to the agents by the high command was to act without interfering.

A task force was created and PF troops in conjunction with civilian and military police were given carte blanche to act on that mission and within hours they invaded the place where the second largest faction of Pará existed. Upon arriving suddenly, they received no resistance and easily entered the territory dominated by the trafficker, because there was a peace agreement between them and the authorities, Nine Fingers did not allow discord between his men and the police.

Surprised by the sudden arrival of the agents, all with guns drawn, he wanted to know what was happening and what he heard from the police officers' mouths perplexed him.

— We have been ordered to take into custody the three elements that you keep here

— I don't know what elements you refer to

— Don't be a beggar, man, we received the safe information that The Red Skull and his two cronies take shelter in this place under your protection, so try again to collaborate with us and avoid further complications between us and your people

— Don't threaten us, Captain!

— It's not about threats, I just ask you to collaborate

— I know you are willing to do anything to carry out your orders.

85

But I will not betray a great friend

— So confirm the information we received, do the three miscreants really hide here?

— Captain, look around you, we are four times bigger than you. So a confrontation at this point would be suicide

— Now who threatens us is you

— It was just a warning to get real. Now take your men and withdraw from my territory, captain, tell your superiors that I refuse to cooperate peacefully with them this time, I will not easily hand over my friend

— Very well, but know that your decision will have serious consequences

— I'll know how to deal with them

The policemen withdrew from there breathing threats, but they could do nothing.

Since the order they received was to try to resolve everything peacefully without a direct confrontation against the drug dealer and his men. Soon after the Nine Fingers left, he ordered his friend and his two companions to be taken out of hiding and explained what happened in greater detail.

— So you mean they were warned of our presence here at your house? But by whom?

— It seems that I was wrong to think that there were no mice here, friend

— I think so

— But don't worry, I will locate and punish this wretch

— And how will you identify this traitor?

— That's easy. Watch and Learn

The drug dealer ordered all of his men who were security guards to assemble in a large space located in the vicinity of his home, placing them in line, demanding that the whistleblower manifest himself to account for his act or everyone would be punished. As he didn't get any positive answer, he drew his gun and killed one of them with a bullet through his forehead.

Seeing the colleague with his skull blown out, the others realized that the boss was serious and feared too much of the account, however they could do nothing to appease their anger.

Because they knew nothing about it. In this way, another of them was killed with a shot in the chest and at close range, leading the rest to ask for mercy from the angry bandit who shouted profanity and demanded that the traitor be reported by his companions, but nobody seemed to know who it was.

A third party started to have the barrel of a pistol pointed at his face and at that moment Nego Teo, a trusted man of the Nine Fingers spoke out in defense of the same. It was his youngest brother who was improperly placed in the pack.

Without understanding exactly the friend's posture Nine fingers wanted to know why he would be defending the lackey, what is the reason for such compassion, it was there that he became aware of their kinship and his anger rose much more, because Nego Teo knew that he did not agreed with relatives acting together in the faction and felt betrayed by the partner in the crime.

— But what an unfortunate betrayal that was on your part, Teo, aren't you aware that I don't agree with that?

— Yes, I know that, but it was that he was in serious trouble and needed to disappear from the streets for a while, so I decided to put him here with us to stay safe. I'm sorry boss

— Was it not this unfortunate person who reported us to the police?

— No, he's not snitch, boss! Can you believe he wouldn't do that

— Well I think he may have done it to clean up with the Guys out there

— Please, boss, let him go, spare his life

Nine Fingers, held the edge of the boy's shirt and told him to kneel, then looked at Nego Téo and told him to say goodbye to the unfortunate man. Knowing the criminal's merciless character and knowing that he was serious, he decided to negotiate his brother's life in order to free him from certain death.

— Let him go, boss, and I will hand him the traitor

— So you knew who the bastard was all the time and remained silent?

— I told you, let him go and point out who the snitch is

— Well then go on talking, you bastard, or I'll delete that kid right now!

— Promise me to let him go

— I am not obliged to promise you anything you bastard, liar and coward, speak at once or he dies!

— It was me, boss, I told the feds that The Red Skull was here! Okay, I said, let my brother go and then do whatever you want with me!

— Why do you, traitor, have the courage to say that during all these years on my side you were nothing but a fucking snitch, betraying my confidence and still think you can appeal for the life of this sucker? For I will give you what you deserve. You will be crushed like the worm you are, but first I will make you pay for the pain of your betrayal, damn you!

At that very moment he squeezes the trigger and the sound of the shot echoes in place. The projectile went through the young man's skull, which was shaken in the thick grass, causing Nego Téo to despair. Crying, he threw himself on the body of the youngest brother, who was already lifeless.

—- Miserable, why didn't you just do this to me?

— Sending you a bullet in the face would be too little in the face of what you did to me, this pain will make you feel the disappointment it caused me, you bastard!

The trafficker burned with hatred and ordered him to start the traitor's sentence

— Take this bastard from here, tie him to that wooden pole!

His order was immediately obeyed and in a few minutes the snitch was already properly attached to the wooden post and surrounded by several pieces of rotten boards, cardboard and other flammable junk.

After addressing him with low-level words and accusing him of allowing the death of some of the men, who were innocent, being silent even aware that he deserved the punishment, he ordered them to light the fire so that he would be burned alive in the presence of all.

As the fire grew and the flames cooked his trapped and inert body, it was only possible for him to scream and move his head in despair, everyone who watched that act of enormous impiety was even more frightened to commit the same insanity in the future.

Except The Red Skull and his two paces that, of course, were already used to similar or even worse situations. The macabre session ended, everyone reoccupied their posts and the four went to drink tequila in the large and luxurious room of the house where nine fingers lived, met there and discussed the future of friends Skull.

Fourth Part

Paying For Your Mistakes

Nine Fingers attitude in refusing to collaborate with the authorities and handing over the friend "Red Skull" and his cronies caused enormous indignation to the Civil and Federal Military Command who decided to order an unexpected attack on the criminal faction, as they concluded that he disrespected the agreement that existed between them when challenging them.

Thus, when they least expected it, a huge number of police invaded the perimeter dominated by the drug dealer and began to exchange shots at the perpetrators who guarded the place, leading Nine Fingers to call other allies who came to his aid immediately. However, despite having been in a number considered they could not contain the more than three hundred police officers who used large caliber weapons in the action that took a very long time to complete. The two friends were still talking at that time.

Discussing what means would be used for The Red Skull and his cronies to flee from Brazil to Paraguay without being noticed. When they were surprised by the troops. During the confrontation, several criminals were killed and some of the invaders were injured, because the outlaws outnumbered the defense and had to surrender.

"Red Skull" and his partners still fought against the troops, helping to defend the ground with the colleagues who helped him, but in order not to be killed they opted in surrender. Captured and taken to the Command, they were handed over to the authorities who took him to one of the PF cells until the Justice decided the future of the criminals.

A week later, all the prisoners were already seated in the dock and being judged for their crimes as mandated by the Law, The Skull and the others were sentenced each according to the judges and the Jury considered it convenient, taking into account the crimes committed against the society and the victims they executed.

The commercialization and distribution of drugs in the state and the destruction of public assets during the vandalism practiced days ago by the city streets. Red Skull was sentenced to twenty years of imprisonment in a closed regime and without the right to appeal by his lawyers.

As he had a lot of money obtained by selling tons of narcotics during the several years working in the life of the crime, it was easy to hire defenders. That they endeavored to try to reduce their sentence, because even as a convict he had this right. But, unfortunately, the judges were adamant in dealing with this case and even after dozens of attempts made by the defense he remained imprisoned and without hope of having his sentence reduced.

Within the maximum security penitentiary the bandit was placed in a cell in a cell separate from the others, while his two partners were together with other highly dangerous prisoners and this led to them being harassed by them, as they knew them of criminal life and some were your foes since a long time ago.

This situation worsened to the point that the two were seriously attacked inside the cell and tortured several times by the other prisoners, which led the prison leadership to transfer them to another pavilion, where they could certainly pay their sentence more safely, but they were mistaken about that.

In that wing of the jail there were other even more dangerous foes and as soon as they got there they were beaten to death. Aware of what happened to the Skull colleagues, he feared for his life and expected the worst. Every day, when all the detainees went out to sunbathe in the large courtyard of the penal house, he kept his distance from the other prisoners.

So he acted to avoid any aggression, but they gathered in packs and surrounded him in an air of threat. One morning, when they met there, he realized that they were plotting his death. One of the condemned armed himself with something sharp and tried to approach him with the intention of hurting him, but he did not give any chance to the enemy who, even though he was unable to put into practice his intention, persisted in attacking him by surprise. After sunbathing, they were taken to their cells and at lunch time they again met in the spacious cafeteria.

Skull was young, but smart and very perceptive, immediately realizing the treacherous plan of the other criminals. Thus, he remained on constant alert against any onslaught by them against his life, placing himself at the end of the line and never failing to watch the rear.

A certain individual who was right in front of him, taking advantage while he was careless just a few seconds turned in his direction and wounded him with a pocket knife, but not as deeply as he intended. This made the terrible killer show those who wanted his death that even though he was a young man and apparently fragile, he did not fear his threats.

His large physique allowed him to grab his opponent by the neck and disarm him. He held his arms back and then buried his face in the hot food tray, drawing a deep cry of pain out of it.

Then he punched his stomach, his face, the low places and to complement the damage he used his big and strong hands to break his neck. All the other detainees watched from a distance, no one got in the fight as the rules of the factions that operated inside the penal house governed.

Everything lasted only a few minutes and there was no time for jailers or police officers who worked inside the prison to prevent the crime, when they arrived at the scene it was too late to prevent the offender from being killed. From then on, the other detainees began to respect the novice and to know that facing him would not be an easy task.

As a result, the trafficker's lawyers advised him to avoid getting involved again in any other confrontation with any other prisoner, in order to convince the authorities to reduce his sentence, which he agreed without discussing.

After earning the respect of his cellmates, he even formed some friendships and found support from the faction leaders who commanded everything there, facilitating their coexistence.

Two years after his arrest and due to the good behavior presented in the penal house, the lawyers managed to give the judges the right to appeal the sentence. Judge Ivonete Santiago of the Second Criminal Court of the Capital Court of Justice accepted the claims of the defenders. He then ordered that a new hearing be opened.

To judge the case and the result obtained was satisfactory for the defendant who managed to reduce his sentence by fifty percent, but still in a closed regime. His effort to stay out of confusion inside the jail earned him the right to work cleaning the prison unit and after serving the fifth consecutive year of his conviction, he was given the right to a semi-open regime.

Leading him to buy a luxury apartment in a of the noble neighborhoods of the city with the fortune that he had acquired in the life of the crime and that was not confiscated by the Justice, because he kept all his patrimony in the name of oranges, as the entrepreneurs Martins, Claudio and Maurício who moved their millions through several companies cargo transportation, grain deposits, beverages and other forms of investments.

Outside the prison he used the day to rejoin his former partners and become familiar with the business and the night he returned to his cell. In a short time Pedro, formerly The Red Skull, now twenty-seven years old, completely changed and decided not to get involved in crime anymore and the sale of drugs became an important businessman.

There were still some years of sentence to be paid, but due to the beautiful example of social evolution presented by the former criminal, justice granted him a Habeas Corpus. And he was allowed to finish reporting to society for his crimes under an open regime.

In this period in which he conquered freedom again Pedro had already learned all the tricks of the business world and was doing extremely well in business alongside his partners. He abandoned the old practice of crime and was determined to start a family, with an enormous desire to be a father.

He swore that he would act differently from the father he never knew. His purpose was to be a true friend, protector and he would always be present in their daily lives, he would not allow them to be humiliated by other boys at school or elsewhere for not having a father. In this way, he devoted himself fully to organizing himself and building a base where he could wait for that hopeful day.

Final part

The Realization of a Dream

The sad and unhappy childhood, made under extreme poverty, the abandonment of the father, the sudden death of the mother and due to the criticisms made by schoolmates for being an orphan boy and lacking in affection made him grow up and even in his adolescence to make wrong friendships , following tortuous paths until he became the biggest criminal in the state where he was born.

Similarly, years spent in prison, inside that filthy and cold cell made him rethink his values, profoundly changing his way of looking at life. When he left there, he decided to completely change his reality and started to dream about the possibility of finding someone special who could live by his side and help him to know the happiness he never had the chance to experience before. His new existence was based on a lot of work and planning for better days, always in the late afternoon he used to take his car of refinement and go.

He usually went somewhere where he can reflect on what he most wants to achieve. That night, fate took him to the port located near the old neighborhood where he had lived as a child and spent the last few moments with his mother before leaving.

The day ended while he was distracted in his thoughts, watching the serenity of the waters and the darkness of the night finally dominated the brightness of the sun that dazzled behind the trees and the small hills that surrounded the river located in front of him, it was like if that farewell of the greatest star took his soul with him.

He lived the ecstasy of admiring the sunset, when a character appears out of nowhere and passes right before his gaze full of admiration, arousing his complete interest. He could not deny that he felt empty, with the need to be able to count on a female company to help him escape from that terrible loneliness that insistently accompanied him.

Especially in the early hours, when it all came down to an unbearable silence, where only the four corners of that wide witnessed his dismay. The girl passed at least two meters from the place where he was sitting, admiring the emptiness around him. His long red hair matched his tall stature. His white skin reflected in the dark that the street lamps struggled to dominate.

Suddenly their eyes met and a sudden smile broke out on his lips. And he couldn't hide the charm. Then the laughter corresponded, the gleam in the eye, the seduction, was dominated by passion. She went ahead and the shy boy just followed her steps from a distance, with immense admiration.

Finally, the beautiful young woman sits down at one of the tables in the cafeteria located nearby and without realizing himself, he was overcome with impetus and headed towards her. He boldly approaches and sits next to the unknown woman announcing himself without being invited.

— Good night, I'm Pedro!

She looks at him seriously and tries to understand that bold invasion of his privacy. He tries to compose himself.

— Sorry, I think I rushed. I saw her pass by now and I was enchanted by her beauty, so I took the initiative to come and talk to her

She smiles and then introduces herself to the unknown.

— My name is Vera, the pleasure is all mine

— So, allow me to keep you company?

— I would love to, but I will warn you that I expect some friends and they are a real pain, they love to spoil pleasure — Both laugh at the comical situation.

— Okay, as soon as they leave

— I advise you to do this

They love to make fun of other people that they consider not to belong to the same social level

— I understand. But is your name Vera?

— Yes, Elisabeth!

— In the past I had a friend at school with that name

— Were they good friends?

— Actually she was more for my guardian angel than for friend

Both again exchange laughter.

— Is your name really ...?

— Pedro, Pedro from Saints!

The young woman is silent for a few seconds, staring at the boy who remained motionless there, in front of her, and babbled a few words afterwards:

— I do not believe...

— Don't you believe what?

— Is that you...

— What about me?

— You are that boy that my classmates used to beat up at school, when we were still teenagers

Now it was his turn to be amazed at such awareness.

— Will see? Beth from school, is you?

The two young men start laughing non-stop in the absurd way they were unable to recognize each other right away.

— My goodness, how crazy, have we changed so much?

— Well, at least you changed, stopped being that girl full of freckles and became that beauty queen that enchanted my eyes!

— Ah, so you remember I was a freckle? Sometimes it felt like you never paid attention to me

— And how could you with those brutes watching you all the time?

— True, they were just a bunch of ogres

— But apparently you are still together, the same group to this day

— Yeah, I ended up dating Edinaldo

— Wow, that brute who was always beating me?

— So, we all changed schools and went to study right in the same room, there in the other school, then we continue together

— Did you find another punching bag over there?

— Not at all, the scolding of their parents at that time resulted in a huge beating and the guys didn't want to get up to school anymore. But you followed a very dangerous course.

You have become a terrible drug dealer hunted by the police and marked with death. I was never able to understand why you chose to follow this path

— Sometimes life corners us to the point that we are forced to walk through dark places

— This is no excuse to become what you have become or to do what you have done. You stole, tortured and killed innocent people, trafficked and took many young people and teenagers to the world of drugs that they will never be able to get out of. I'm sorry, but it turned out to be a real monster!

— I'm sorry, but at first I didn't realize how bitter you are with me

— It is not bitterness but disappointment

— I'm sorry, but I can't erase the past

— Unfortunately that is the most true, but that's okay, I won't be here throwing you in the face of the mistakes you made. After all, you have already paid with the Justice for the crimes committed. And now, what are your plans for the future?

— Getting married, building a family, having lots of children ...

— Wow, and who is the one who won your heart so deeply?

— I don't know, maybe someone who has lived in it for a long time and I didn't even notice

First there is a deep silence between the two who exchanged an intense look.

Then a slight smile ended the conversation that left the girl confused. An imported, luxurious and exquisite car parks very close to the place where the two friends talk and four muscular elements descend and the taller kisses the girl on the lips.

— Hi honey, sorry for the delay

— Okay, while I waited for you, look who I had the pleasure of meeting again after so many years

The four young look at each other and demonstrate ignorance of the figure present

— Who is that?

— Aren't you recognizing?

— Never seen before - replied one of them

— Neither do I - added Luís, the youngest

— Come on guys, give our friend a better look!

— We already talked, Vera, we don't know who it is!

— It's Pedro, Edinaldo, that boy from school that you used to be martyred for being an orphan

— Jesus Christ, you are "The Red Skull", the biggest drug dealer in history!

— Edinaldo was terrified

— No, that one doesn't exist anymore!

109

Today I became a good man, rest assured

— It is very easy for you to leave behind all the barbarities you committed and move on, but for the relatives of the victims who were martyred by you, the pain will be forever! — Warns Luís

— Each one becomes what life allows him to be, I may have become a monster, but it was people like you who contributed to this happening

— Look at the guy, man, now you want to blame me for choosing to be a bad guy on our backs? — Disdain Paulo

Pedro's blood boils in his veins and for a few seconds he wanted to fight back the playboy's irony at the height of the affront he received, however, he had the strength to remain calm and not further complicate his relationship with Elisabeth, who was already quite disappointed with your past attitudes.

— I'm not putting any blame on anyone, but we all here know how much I was martyred by you and how painful the humiliation was

— Ah, come on my brother, that was just a child's prank. We were all kids and we had no idea if our behavior was affecting your head or letting you down

— Well, Edinaldo, as the saying goes, whoever forgets, but whoever gets beaten always remembers — Pedro added

— Do you want to know something? Let us leave these disagreements and hurts behind.

O Caveira Vermelha - Romance

The past can no longer be fixed, however, the present can be corrected. Hold hands and form the good friendship that should have existed in our childhood and we will all be at peace — Opinioned the girl

Despite the momentary hesitation, the four boys finally ended up holding hands and closing the agreement to start a great friendship and then went to a very fine restaurant to have a dinner with friends to write a new story in their lives.

From that day on, the five started to walk together, going to various places of entertainment and the union between them only increased. Pedro became a renowned businessman in the social environment and, along with his partners, he made great financial progress. A year after reconciliation with former schoolmates Edinaldo died in an accident involving his car and a bus on one of the highways that connected the capital to one of the many beaches on the coast.

With his death Vera was very sad and spent some months in prison at the maternal grandparents' house in the city of Salinas, where she refused to receive even the visit of relatives and close friends who had the intention of comforting her. However, over time she ended up settling for what happened and returned to Belem where she met again with the three friends.

— We were happy with your return.

My dear, we were very concerned about you — Advance Paulo

— Thanks. It really wasn't easy to overcome the pain of our loss, Edinaldo was not only my boyfriend, but our friend, a brother to us all

— Without a doubt, especially for you who lived with him since childhood and have always been together — added the newest member of the group

— Yes, Pedro, you are absolutely right — Luís agrees

— But now enough of sadness and lamentation, he certainly wouldn't want us to stay here whining forever

— Realistic as it was would like us to continue our lives with joy and not with tears in our eyes and that is what we will do, we will give our friend and brother reasons to smile there in heaven

— That's it, Elisabeth, no regrets! — Supported Joaquim

Day after day the group remained united and in their spare time they were always in the company of each other and this brought Pedro and Elisabeth closer together. He had already realized that he was attracted to his friend since the first reunion, but he respected the fact that she is committed to Edinaldo. However, since she would have been practically a widow not long ago, nothing would have stopped him from confessing his feelings to her, however, he found it more convenient to let the wound of his loss heal enough. To consider his declaration of love.

It was on a rainy winter afternoon, when for the first time only the two young men were gathered in a cottage in the square called Republic, located in the center of the city, waiting for the others who coincidentally did not appear that Pedro decided to declare himself to Elisabeth, during the crash of a heavy thunderstorm.

Since she was a child, the girl trembled before the typical thunderstorms of the intense winter rains that fell in that region and on that day it could not be different, as soon as it flashed and the thunder boom seemed to break the sky from side to side she threw herself in the arms of her friend and hugged him tightly with eyes closed, letting out a cry of dread. The boy allows her to grab him and responds to the hug with intense protection.

Seconds before they talked about the delay of other friends and he was looking for a way to say that he loved her, she realized that the young man wanted to say something to her and was not stupid to the point of noticing his interest, but hoped that the attitude would come from him, valuing him. if as a woman. But when they came face to face, looking each other in the eye and he was going to tell her about his feelings, nature disturbs him with a loud crash. However, despite everything he did not give up and took advantage of the moment of fright suffered by the girl and after hugging her tightly, giving her the necessary warmth para se to warm up in your arms.

He then looks steadily into the depths of her eyes and kisses her with intense madness. The kiss is reciprocated and they both surrender to the desire that for so long burned in their souls and grew in two hearts in love, because she has always loved him since she was a girl.

The revelation that they were together and intended to get married soon was a big surprise for friends who did not even imagine that union was possible, since Elisabeth and Edinaldo were always very passionate, but this surprise was soon undone and in a few months they were already scheduled wedding and all other arrangements for the marriage bond were already underway, as a large party was waiting for hundreds of guests. The couple exchanged rings on the tenth day of September of that year, in the month when the flowers gave off the greatest perfume.

Shortly thereafter Pedro, the former "Red Skull", a common drug dealer, murderer, rapist, enemy number one of the Civil, Military and Federal police, who for years caused panic and terror throughout the state of Pará, transformed into a good man after paying his debt to society became a father for the first time.

Estela was the name given to the couple's first daughter and, a year later, it was the turn of son Pedro, a name chosen by Elisabeth, so that he could honor his father.

Friend and eternal companion. The young businessman kept his promise and dedicated himself totally to the family he received from God, they never lacked attention, love and protection. Her children were never humiliated at school due to their father's absence or because they lived in complete misery, because he provided for everything.

— I want to thank you for everything

— No, I thank you for providing me with so much happiness

— Thank you for the true love, the affection, the care, the zeal you have for us

— Thank you for the children you gave me, for this beautiful family that we formed — He kisses her with intense passion

— THE END —

Lightning Source UK Ltd.
Milton Keynes UK
UKRC022224210720
366677UK00024B/102